BLACKBERRY FARM

SPORTS DAY AT BLACKBERRY FARM

Jane Pilgrim

This edition first published in the United Kingdom in 2000 by
Brockhampton Press
20 Bloomsbury Street
London WC1B 3QA
a member of the Caxton Publishing Group

Designed and Produced for Brockhampton Press by
Open Door Limited
80 High Street, Colsterworth, Lincolnshire, NG33 5JA

Illustrator: F. Stocks May
Colour separation: GA Graphics Stamford

Title: BLACKBERRY FARM, Sports Day at Blackberry Farm
ISBN: 1-84186-048-4

SPORTS DAY AT BLACKBERRY FARM

Jane Pilgrim

Illustrated by F. Stocks May

BROCKHAMPTON PRESS

One summer day Ernest Owl said to his school: "Listen, everybody. We will have a Sports Day soon." And everybody was very excited.

Ernest Owl went to see Mr
Nibble and Emily the Goat.
"Please, will you both help me
with my Sports Day?" he said. And
Emily and Mr Nibble were very
pleased to help.

Emily and Mr Nibble went off to
make a plan. And they planned to
have running and jumping and
rolling and an egg-and-spoon race.

Ernest Owl wrote the
programmes and Joe Robin
delivered them.

Everyone at Blackberry Farm began to get ready for Sports Day. Mrs Nibble made new shorts for Rosy, Posy and Christopher. But poor Christopher had hurt his paw and would not be able to run.

Even Henrietta, Henry the
Pig's sister, came with all her
children. They met Mrs Squirrel
and Hazel on the way. Mrs
Squirrel was very pleased because
she had not seen Henrietta for a
long time. "How your children
have grown!" she said.

Mrs Nibble provided tea for
everyone and Lucy Mouse helped
to pour out. They were very busy,
because everyone who lived at
Blackberry Farm was there.

At last they were all ready. Mr Nibble started the races, Emily saw who won and Ernest Owl wrote it all down. Hazel won the first race and Martha Lamb came second. Mrs Squirrel shouted so loud that she lost her voice.

When the time came for
jumping, Rosy and Posy came first
equal and Mr Nibble was very
proud. "I could not jump so high
when I was young," he said. And
Mrs Nibble was so excited that she
knocked over a jug of milk.

Then as a surprise, Ernest Owl said: "Now we will have a hopping race." And this was won by Mother Hen's little daughter, Mary, who hopped very fast indeed.

The egg-and-spoon race was won
by Walter Duck's three children,
William, Watney and Wallace. They
were so very good at holding their
spoons in their beaks.

Henrietta's little pigs had spent a
long time practising rolling and
they all came in first.

At the end Ernest Owl gave the prizes and Christopher had a special one because he had hurt his paw.

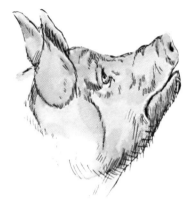

Then Henry the Pig shouted:
"Three cheers for Ernest Owl and
Emily and Mr Nibble for a
wonderful Sports Day!" and all the
animals at Blackberry Farm
cheered and agreed that they had
not enjoyed themselves so much
for a long time.